A DRAGON CHRISTMAS
THINGS TO MAKE AND DO

A DRAGON CHRISTMAS
THINGS TO MAKE AND DO
WRITTEN AND ILLUSTRATED BY
LOREEN LEEDY
HOLIDAY HOUSE · NEW YORK

For my brothers and sisters
RUTH ANNE, ROLLEAN, VIRGINIA, AND ROBERT

Library of Congress Cataloging-in-Publication Data

Leedy, Loreen.
A dragon Christmas.

Summary: A caveful of dragons busily make decorations,
cards, and tasty treats for Christmas, fill the night
with caroling, and enjoy breakfast and presents on
Christmas morning.
[1. Christmas—Fiction.   2. Dragons—Fiction.
3. Stories in rhyme]   I. Title.
PZ8.3.L4995Ds   1988   [E]   88-4635
ISBN 0-8234-0716-0

Ma Dragon grins and shouts with cheer,
"Christmastime is almost here!
Dragons, grab your tape and glue,
Hurry, there's a lot to do!"

Each dragon gathers odds and ends
For making cards to mail to friends.

SPONGE-STAMP CARDS

1. Draw design on sponge with marker and cut out.

2. Fold construction paper in half to make card. (Cut in half to make smaller cards.)

3. Dip sponge-stamp into puddle of paint. Print card. Let dry.

PUZZLE CARDS

1. Draw a Christmas picture and write a greeting on construction-paper. Color with crayons or markers.

2. Cut into 8 or 10 pieces, place in envelope, and mail.

Display cards that you receive by attaching with paper clips to ribbon or string.

COLLAGE CARDS

1. Cut apart old greeting cards. Gather bits of ribbon, lace, gift wrap, glitter, etc.

2. Arrange to make a pleasing design. Glue to a folded construction-paper card. Let dry.

FOAM-PRINT CARDS

1. Cut the sides off a foam tray. (Grocery stores often package meat and fruit on foam trays.)

2. Use a blunt pencil to draw lines and shapes.

3. Brush on thin layer of paint. Press tray firmly onto a folded construction-paper card. Lift carefully. Let print dry.

Decorations everywhere
Give the cave a festive air.

MERRY CHRISTMAS BANNER

1. Draw letters on construction-paper.

2. Cut out letters.

3. Tape string to back of letters.

4. Hang banner with tape or tacks.

SNOWFLAKES

1. On white typing paper, trace around a large can. Cut out circle.

2. Fold circle in half.

3. Fold in half again.

4. Cut out triangles, half-circles, squares, and other shapes.

5. Carefully unfold. Tape snowflakes to windows and walls.

TISSUE PAPER WREATH

1. Cut center out of a paper plate. Punch hole on edge.

2. Cut tissue paper into 1½ inch squares.

3. Fold each tissue square around the eraser end of a pencil. Dip in glue.

4. Press tissue onto paper plate. Keep adding tissue until plate is covered. Let dry.

5. Leave wreath white or add drips of food coloring. Add bow if desired. Use hole to hang.

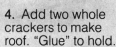

CRACKER COTTAGE CENTERPIECE

1. Stuff an empty cereal box with paper. Cover with foil. Tape ends.

2. Use 2 whole graham crackers to make side walls. Break a whole cracker in half to make square end walls. Use white frosting as "glue." (See page 21.)

3. Break off two opposite corners from half cracker, tilt, and "glue" inside end wall. Repeat for other end.

4. Add two whole crackers to make roof. "Glue" to hold.

5. Spread frosting "snow" on roof. Use frosting to glue on construction-paper windows and door.

6. Spread out drifts of frosting "snow." Twigs make "trees" and evergreen sprigs make "bushes."

The dragons cut and paste with glee
To make the trimmings for the tree.

FOIL ICICLES

1. Tear strip of foil about 4 inches wide.

2. With fingertips, firmly crush foil into a stick.

3. Shape stick into zigzag or spiral. Bend one end to form hook.

SHELL ORNAMENTS

1. Fold a 6-inch piece of thin twine in half. Glue to inside of small shell. Let dry.

2. Decorate with gold paint, or glue on ribbon bows. Let dry.

SNOWBIRDS

1. Draw a bird on construction-paper or poster board.

2. Color bird with markers or crayons.

3. Cut out bird.

4. Staple piece of wire or twist-tie to back side. Wrap wire around tree branch.

5. Make a whole flock!

COOKIE CUTTER ORNAMENTS

1. Place cookie cutter on folded sheet of construction-paper. Draw around it.

2. Cut out the two shapes.

3. Glue a 6-inch loop of string on inside edge of one shape. Apply glue around entire edge. Press two shapes together.

4. Decorate by gluing on bits of paper, ribbon, sequins, etc. Use a fine-tip marker for details. Let dry before hanging.

GIFT-WRAP GARLAND

1. Cut strips from wrapping paper, about 1 inch by 5 inches.

2. Tape or glue one strip into a circle.

3. Add another strip.

4. Keep adding strips to make long chain.

5. Drape garland around Christmas tree.

Ornaments hang high and low,
Snowflakes and wild mistletoe.

12

The busy dragons work with care,
Making special gifts to share.

House Doorstop

1. Wash out half-gallon carton. Fill with sand or pebbles. Use masking tape to seal top and cover side openings.

2. Place carton on felt. Trace around side and peak with pen. Cut out.

3. Spread glue on carton. Press felt in place. Repeat steps 2 and 3 for all four sides and bottom.

4. Cut felt roof in one piece, allowing to overhang slightly. Glue into place.

5. Use black ball-point pen to draw stones on "walls."

6. Cut doors, shutters, and windows from felt. Attach with glue.

Bookmarks

1. Cut strip of felt about 1 inch wide and 8 inches long.

2. Cut a heart from another color of felt and glue to one end of strip.

Try a flower or an abstract design

or a bird

or a bear face

or a star

or an initial.

COUPON BOOK

1. Cut 9 rectangles from construction-paper (3 inches by 4 inches).

2. Punch hole in upper left corner of each coupon.

3. Use markers or crayons to write a chore you will perform, on each coupon.

4. Add a picture of the task, if desired.

5. Thread ribbon or string through holes and tie.

ANIMAL MAGNET SET

1. Coil a pipe cleaner around a large marker (at least 5/8 inch in diameter). Remove coil.

2. Twist up one end of pipe cleaner to make tail.

3. Cut out animal head and rear from felt. (Make them at least 1 inch across.) Glue on felt-scrap nose.

4. Add details with fine-tip markers.

5. Glue head and rear to body. Let dry. Glue magnet to rear. Let dry.

6. Make cats, dogs, lions, elephants, etc.

First one step and then another,
Creating presents for each other.

PRINTED T-SHIRT

1. Spread out newspapers. Place layer of papers inside shirt, so paint won't soak through.

2. Use special fabric paint to print shirt with sponges (p. 6) or foam trays (p. 7). Let dry.

3. Try an allover design or just decorate sleeves and neck

or make stripes.

COLORED TISSUE VASE

1. Wash and dry a clear glass bottle. (Remove labels by soaking in warm water.)

2. Tear colored tissue into pieces about 1 by 2 inches. (Two different colors will overlap to form third color.)

3. Brush white glue thinned with water onto bottle. Apply tissue piece and brush again with glue.

4. Add tissue until glass is covered. Tissue can be smooth or wrinkled. Let dry.

5. Give bottle another coat of thinned glue. Let dry.

Animal Bank

1. Save an empty food container with straight sides and a plastic lid. Clean inside with soap and water.

2. Have an adult cut a slit in lid about 1 inch by ⅛ inch.

3. Replace lid. Cut a piece of felt to cover container.

4. Spread glue on container. Press felt into place.

5. Cut and glue on felt nose, eyes, feet, ears, etc. Use a fine-tip marker for lines.

Magazine Puppets

1. Find pictures of animals, people, and toys in old magazines. Cut out figure, roughly at first.

2. Spread thin layer of glue on cardboard or poster board. Press cutout down smoothly. Let dry.

3. Cut closely around figure, but don't cut out space between legs. (Base must be wide to be strong.)

4. Glue figure to Popsicle stick. Let dry.

The dragons wrap the gifts up tight,
To hide their handiwork from sight.

LEAF RUBBING GIFT WRAP

Use crayons, white shelf paper, and leaves.
Place leaf under paper and rub crayon over it.
Move leaf and repeat, until paper is covered.

RUBBER STAMP WRAP

Use rubber stamps on white shelf paper. Try a
checkerboard pattern or stripes. Stamp the
ribbon too!

DRIBBLE DRIP PAPER

Spread out plenty of newspapers. Lay sheet of white tissue
paper on top. Sprinkle food coloring or paint thinned with water
all over tissue. Use brush to make squiggly lines. Let dry.

Comic Cutouts

Wrap gift in plain paper. Cut out comics from the newspaper and glue in place. Let dry.

Paper Bag Wrap

Decorate white lunch bags with markers or crayons, placing design on lower half of bag. Wrap gift in tissue paper, put inside bag, and use thick yarn to tie.

Nature Prints

Spread out thick layer of newspapers. Unroll white shelf paper on top. Have an adult cut fruit or vegetable in half. Dip in puddle of paint and print on shelf paper. Let dry. Try mushrooms, apples, potatoes, etc.

Dragons like to gobble sweets
Cookies, cakes, and spicy treats.

PEANUT BUTTER CRITTERS
Preheat oven to 350°F

BEAT
UNTIL — ½ C. peanut butter
FLUFFY   ½ C. butter, softened
          ½ C. sugar
          1 egg

SIFT — 1 C. flour
       ½ tsp. salt
       ½ tsp. baking soda
Add to butter mix to make a soft dough.

Use food coloring to color small portions
of dough. Press bits and balls of dough
together on ungreased cookie sheets
to make all kinds of animals, about
¼ inch thick. Bake 8 to 10 minutes,
cool for a minute on cookie sheet,
then carefully move cookies off to
finish cooling on wire racks.
Makes 2 to 3 dozen critters.

Ask for an adult's permission before cooking and using oven.

Clean up kitchen as you work.

GINGERBREAD CUPCAKES
Preheat oven to 350°F

CREAM — ½ C. butter
½ C. sugar

ADD — ½ C. molasses
½ C. hot water
1 egg

SIFT — 1½ C. flour
1 tsp. baking soda
½ tsp. cinnamon
¼ tsp. ginger
¼ tsp. cloves
¼ tsp. salt
Add to butter mixture.

Spoon into 12 paper-lined muffin cups. Bake for 25 minutes. Frost with SNOWY FROSTING (see below) and decorate with candies. Makes 1 dozen.

SNOWY FROSTING
STIR — 1 C. powdered sugar
UNTIL — 2 tbs. shortening
WELL — 1 tbs. milk
MIXED — ½ tsp. vanilla

21

Families, friends, and neighbors trade
Delicious goodies they have made.

POPCORN SNOWBALLS

HAVE READY – 8 C. popped popcorn
Remove any hard kernels

STIR – ½ C. sugar
½ C. light corn syrup
Cook and stir in large saucepan over medium heat until sugar has dissolved and mixture is bubbly.

ADD – ¼ C. butter
1 tsp. vanilla
Cook 2 more minutes. Remove from heat.

STIR IN – 8 C. popcorn
Allow to cool enough to handle. Put butter on hands and form mixture into 3 inch balls. Place onto waxed paper to harden. Makes 1 dozen.

WHOLE WHEAT OATMEAL NUGGETS

Preheat oven to 350°F

CREAM – ½ C. butter
½ C. brown sugar

ADD – ¼ C. milk
1 egg

SIFT – 1 C. whole-wheat flour
½ tsp. baking soda
½ tsp. cinnamon
Add to butter mixture.

STIR IN – 1 C. rolled oats
½ C. raisins
¼ C. chopped walnuts
Drop small spoonfuls of dough onto cookie sheet. Bake for 8 to 10 minutes. Makes 4 dozen.

SUGAR DROPS
Preheat oven to 375°F

BEAT –
- ¾ C. sugar
- ½ C. vegatable oil
- 1 egg
- ¼ C. milk

SIFT –
- 2 C. sifted flour
- 1 tsp. baking powder
- ½ tsp. salt

Add to sugar mixture to make a thick batter. Drop by spoonfuls onto a greased cookie sheet. Sprinkle each cookie with sugar, then bake for 8 to 10 minutes, until edges are light brown. Makes 4 dozen.

CHOCOLATE & PEANUT BUTTER SANDWICHES
Preheat oven to 375°F

BEAT –
- ½ C. butter
- ¾ C. sugar
- 1 egg
- ½ C. cocoa

SIFT
- 1½ C. flour
- 1 tsp. baking powder

Add to butter mixture. Roll dough into 1 inch balls and place on cookie sheet. Butter a flat-bottomed glass, and dip glass in sugar before flattening each cookie. Bake for 8 to 9 minutes, and cool on wire racks. Spread PEANUT BUTTER FILLING (below) on half of the cookies, then press on the rest of the cookies to make sandwiches. Makes 1½ dozen.

PEANUT BUTTER FILLING

STIR UNTIL MIXED –
- ⅔ C. peanut butter
- ½ C. powdered sugar
- 3 tbs. milk

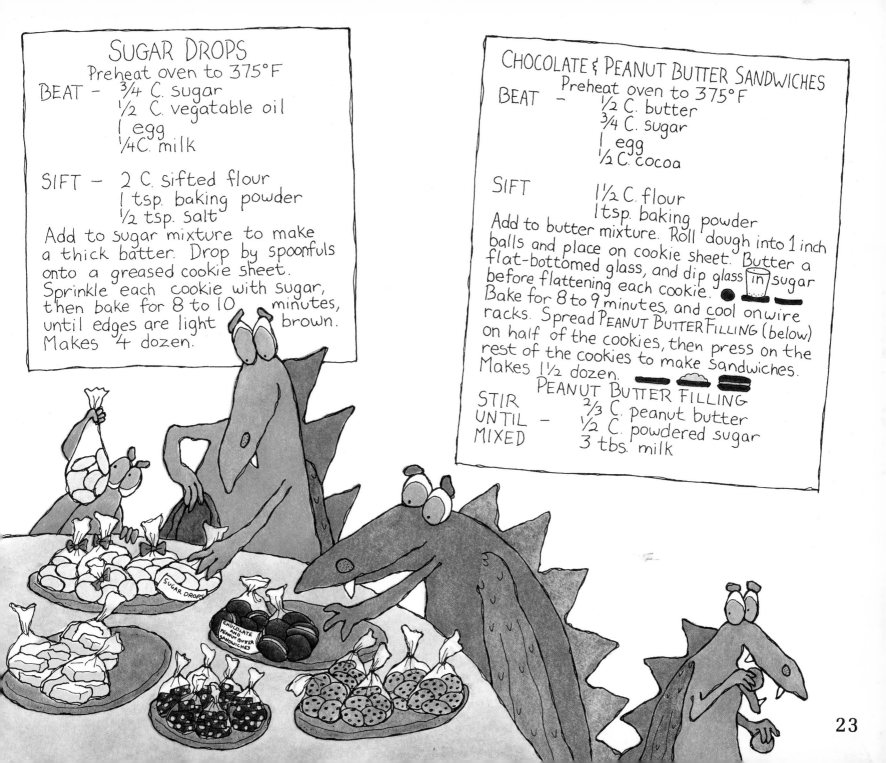

Joyful dragons like to sing.
They fill the night with caroling.

25

A fire is lit, a story read,
Sleepy dragons go to bed.

At sunrise, to the tree they zoom.
Shreds of giftwrap fill the room.

A pancake breakfast starts the day.
The jolly dragons laugh and say,

"A Dragon Christmas is full of fun,
Merry Christmas, everyone!"

PROJECT TIPS

BEFORE YOU BEGIN

1. Read through the directions first.
2. Gather together all the materials. Some can be found around the house or bought at grocery stores. Others, like fabric paint, can be bought at craft or variety stores.
3. Work with a good light source.
4. Spread out newspapers on the work surface and keep a wastebasket nearby.

MATERIALS

1. Paint: acrylic paint works best. Good quality poster paint or tempera paint will work also. Follow directions on the label of special fabric paint for use on clothing.
2. Glue: use a thick, "tacky" white glue, if possible, especially with felt projects.

WHEN YOU FINISH

1. Put everything away. (A shoe box is a good place to store materials.)
2. Wash out your brushes with soap and water. Don't allow acrylic paint to harden.

32